To my brother, Ben
D. M.

For John F.
S. M.

First published 1998 by Walker Books Ltd
87 Vauxhall Walk, London SE11 5HJ

This edition published 1999

2 4 6 8 10 9 7 5 3

Text © 1998 David Martin
Illustrations © 1998 Susan Meddaugh

This book has been typeset in Stone Informal.

Printed in Hong Kong/China

British Library Cataloguing in Publication Data
A catalogue record for this book is
available from the British Library.

ISBN 0-7445-6346-1

THIS WALKER BOOK BELONGS TO:

_____

_____

_____

_____

Five Little Piggies

Stories by David Martin

illustrated by Susan Meddaugh

WALKER BOOKS
AND SUBSIDIARIES
LONDON · BOSTON · SYDNEY

This Little Piggy
Went to Market

"Little Piggy, will you go to market? We need eggs and milk and apples," said Mamma Piggy.

"OK," said Little Piggy. And she went to market singing,

"Eggs and milk and apples.
Megs and milk and mapples.
Pegs and pilk and papples."

When she got to the market she said,

On the way home she saw some chickens and cows eating apples.

"Oh, now I remember!" said Little Piggy, and she ran back to the market and bought eggs and milk and apples.

"Mummy, I'm back," said Little Piggy.

"Good. Did you get everything?" said Mamma Piggy.

"Oh, they're delicious pooples," said Mamma Piggy.
"And here's a great big **BUG** for my silly piggy wiggy."

This Little Piggy
Stayed at Home

SPLASH!

Little Piggy spilled his juice.

CRASH!

He dropped his cereal on the floor.

RIP!

His trousers split and all the other little piggies laughed at him.

Mamma Piggy said, "I think you should stay at home with me today." And she sent the others off to school.

All day long Little Piggy and Mamma Piggy cooked and ate and played together.

"We had slopcakes and syrup for lunch!" said Little Piggy when the others came home from school.

The next day, all the other little piggies spilled their juice and dropped their cereal on the floor.

"Mummy, can we stay at home with you today?" they asked.
"Of course you can," said Mamma Piggy.

"Not me," said Little Piggy.
"I'm going to school."

3

This Little Piggy
Had Roast Beef

"Little piggies, come and eat," called Mamma Piggy.

"Not slops again!" said Little Piggy. "Why can't we have roast beef?"

"OK," said Mamma Piggy.
"Here's some roast beef."

"It's good, but
something is missing,"
said Little Piggy.

"Try some potatoes with it,"
said Mamma Piggy.

"It still isn't right," said Little Piggy.

"Here, dump in these bananas your brother sat on," said Mamma Piggy.

"Oh, that's good," said Little Piggy. "Can we put in the rotten eggs from breakfast, too?"

"Yummy!" said Little Piggy, and she threw in last week's soup and a squishy aubergine.

"Now it's perfect. Try some, Mummy!"

"Delicious!" said Mamma Piggy.
"But it tastes like slops to me."
"No," said Little Piggy.
"That's not slops. That's
ROAST BEEF!"

I want roast beef, too!

Me too! Me too!

4

This Little Piggy Had None

One day Mamma Piggy went shopping and came home with treats for everyone.

But Little Piggy
dropped his
ice-cream

and his
balloons
flew away

and then Little Piggy
had none.

Little Piggy cried and cried.

"MUMMY!
I want
ice-Cream!
I want
balloons!"

Suddenly the other little piggies began to cry, too. And they cried even harder.

"Uh, oh. You four piggies all have chicken-pox," said Mamma Piggy. "But not you, Little Piggy. You haven't got any spots, NONE!"

"Mummy! I **WANT** spots!" said Little Piggy.
"OK," said Mamma Piggy. "You can have spots, too."

5

This Little Piggy Cried
Wee Wee Wee
All the Way Home

Little Piggy was playing with the piggies next door.

Suddenly she got up and started running.
"Wee wee wee," she cried.

"What's the matter, Little Piggy?" asked her sister.

"Why are you crying?" asked her brother.

"Did you hurt yourself, Little Piggy?" asked Mamma Piggy.
But Little Piggy just ran faster and cried,
"Wee wee wee," all the way home.

Then she cried,
"Wee
wee
wee,"
all the
way up
the stairs.

And she cried, "Wee wee wee," all the way to the bathroom.

"*OH !*" said Little Piggy when she came out. "That feels better. I really had to go!"

MORE WALKER PAPERBACKS
For You to Enjoy

LITTLE CHICKEN CHICKEN
by David Martin/Sue Heap

Everyone laughs at Little Chicken Chicken when she makes a tightrope out of a piece of string and says her black stones fell out of a thundercloud. But when thunder and lightning begin, Little Chicken Chicken's magic goes down a storm! The illustrations are by the creator of *Cowboy Baby*, Winner of the 1998 Smarties Book Prize (Under 5 Category).

"Dare to be different is the message of this uplifting tale about the triumph of the imagination." *The Independent*

0-7445-5236-2   £4.99

ONCE UPON A TIME
by Vivian French/John Prater

A little boy tells of his "dull" day, while all around a host of favourite nursery characters act out their stories.

"The pictures are excellent, the telegraphic text perfect, the idea brilliant. We have here a classic, I'm sure, with an author-reader bond as strong as *Rosie's Walk*." *Books for Keeps*

0-7445-3690-1   £4.99

GOOD ZAP, LITTLE GROG
by Sarah Wilson/Susan Meddaugh

"Zoodle oop, little Grog," sings little Grog's mother at the start of another fun-filled day. The ooglets are tuzzling, the glipneeps are jumping, the smibblets are giggling – and so will you when you read this wonderful nonsense rhyme!

"As imaginative as anything dreamt up by Mr Lear… Here's a picture book which would delight the tinies, and inspire junior poets." *The School Librarian*

0-7445-4068-2   £5.99

Walker Paperbacks are available from most booksellers, or by post from B.B.C.S., P.O. Box 941, Hull, North Humberside HU1 3YQ

24 hour telephone credit card line 01482 224626

To order, send: Title, author, ISBN number and price for each book ordered, your full name and address, cheque or postal order payable to BBCS for the total amount and allow the following for postage and packing:
UK and BFPO: £1.00 for the first book, and 50p for each additional book to a maximum of £3.50.
Overseas and Eire: £2.00 for the first book, £1.00 for the second and 50p for each additional book.

Prices and availability are subject to change without notice.